The Girl Who
The Languages

CW00815822

First published in the UK in 2019 by the Emma Press

Originally published in 2012 as *Meitene, kura mācēja visas pasaules valodas* by Pētergailis, in Riga, Latvia

A CIP catalogue record of this book is available from the British Library

Supported by Latvian Writers' Union (*Latvijas Rakstnieku Savienība*) and Ministry of Culture of the Republic of Latvia

Kultūras ministrija

Latvia 100 ▬

Printed in Latvia by Jelgavas tipogrāfija on Munken Polar Rough 120 gsm

ISBN 978-1-912915-09-5

The Emma Press Ltd
Registered in England and Wales, no. 08587072
Website: theemmapress.com
Email: hello@theemmapress.com
Jewellery Quarter, Birmingham, UK

IEVA FLAMINGO

The girl who learned all the languages of the world

Translated by Žanete Vēvere Pasqualini

Illustrated by Chein Shyan Lee

THE EMMA PRESS

Contents (of words learned)

... the very first phrase she wrote on a strip of paper and learnt in all eleven languages was Good day! 8

... the word face 10

... this time, Lela learnt the word pink 12

... then she learnt the word stone 13

... Lela looked up and learnt the word Mum 14

... this time Lela learnt the word Dad 14

... Ice-cream! 15

... Lela looked up and learnt the word money 16

... Lela immediately learnt the word child 18

... then she learnt the word hat 19

... Lela found and learnt the word butterfly 20

... she learnt the word water 22

... she also learnt the word fish 22

... she thought for a while and then taught herself the word bubble 25

... she taught herself the word sad 26

... Lela learnt the word letter 27

... she learnt the word dog 29

... she wrote down the word crow in other languages 29

... she also learnt the word earthworm 30

... she looked up and learnt a new word – sneeze 31

... she learnt the word milk 31

... she also learnt the word strawberry 32

... this time, she learnt the word sweets 48

... she learnt the word ball 48

... straight away she also learnt the word map 49

... she also learnt the word help! 51

... she learnt the word miracle 52

... the first word was fart 53

... then the girls learnt the word poo 54

Who made this book?

About the author 58

An interview with Ieva 59

About the illustrator 61

About the translator 62

An interview with Žanete 63

BONUS BITS

Write your own story 66

Translation station 68

About the Emma Press 70

Also from the Emma Press 71

Also from the Emma Press 73

O*nce upon a time* there was a girl called Lela. She was neither very short nor very tall, with shoulder-length hair she wore pushed back with a headband or hairclip. She was smart and witty, but also a teeny bit stubborn.

Maybe she was a little *too* stubborn at times. If Lela wanted to do something, she would; if not – she wouldn't, simply because of her stubbornness. Lela's mum was called Kathleen and she drew pretty illustrations for children's books, while her dad, Edward, was a diplomat, which made Lela feel very proud. Other dads were builders, teachers, photographers, drivers and bakers, but not *diplomats*. It tripped off the tongue so elegantly, almost like "minister".

As you might expect of a diplomat, Lela's dad was very clever. He could finish almost any crossword. He was always one step ahead of the computer when he played chess. He could do a Rubik's cube without once consulting any formulas. His pancakes were more delicious than Lela's mum's pancakes. And he could speak at least five foreign languages, which meant that he was particularly disappointed when his daughter refused to learn even one.

'Do wild animals ever bother to learn each others' languages?' asked Lela. 'Cats meow; they don't bark. Dogs growl; they wouldn't dream of neighing – that's what horses do! Mice squeak – they don't tweet like birds. And birds cheep; they don't roar like tigers.'

Lela's mum tried everything to convince her, practically standing on her head (although, of course, she didn't), and her dad got as angry as some kind of dictator, even dishing out punishments (she went without any treats or pocket money for a month), but Lela would not budge.

'That's just fine! Sweets rot your teeth, anyway!' And so from that day on, no sugary snacks passed her lips ever again. If she had a craving for something sweet, she went for honey, apples, grapes, cherries, strawberries and oranges instead. She was perfectly happy going without sweets, and her teeth truly did seem healthier and shinier than ever before.

Until one day, when something happened which changed everything...

On that particular day Lela's parents were celebrating. The President himself had recently bestowed upon her dad the highest honour in the land – the Order of the Red Rose – and Lela's mum had organised a special dinner to commemorate the occasion. She booked a table at the city's finest restaurant and, at seven o'clock that evening, ambassadors from other countries started to arrive: some on their own, others with their partners.

To be honest, Lela's mum hadn't really wanted Lela to come to the celebration. She'd said, 'The guests will all be grown-ups, speaking lots of languages you won't understand. I think you'd be better off left with a babysitter!'

But Lela wouldn't take no for an answer, insisting that she really would understand everything. She'd read a whole load of children's encyclopaedias and she knew lots of foreign-sounding words. For example, *croissant, faux pas, lingerie, entrepreneur, rendezvous, delicatessen, kindergarten, macho* and *guerrilla*. Not only that, but she could say 'deoxyribonucleic acid' without even pausing for breath – so who was to say that she wouldn't understand a word at the party?

'There will be ambassadors there from lots of different countries to toast your father and, more often than not, they won't speak our language,' explained her mum over and over again, but Lela wouldn't change her mind. She wasn't going to be taken for a fool.

Lela wore a white dress with red polka dots and a bow tied at the back, a red headband in her hair, and red shoes. Her mum was dressed up to the nines and smelled of freesias and other lovely things. All the guests were dressed very elegantly too, as were the two waiters, who, in their brilliant white shirts and black bow ties, flashed to and fro one after the other, taking care of the guests. While one placed a knife and fork on either side of the plates, the other lit the candles. As the first poured the wine, the second lay the starters on the table.

Lela sat, feeling slightly uneasy, between her mum and a lady in a violet-coloured outfit. Her dad, wearing a black dinner jacket and white shirt, looked a little like a penguin as he sat there in eager discussion with the other penguins. Mum had already asked Lela three times if she needed to go to the bathroom. The lady in violet just stared at her without saying a word – Lela was bored stiff. Words and phrases were flowing all around her, but to her the general hubbub felt like a mix of meaningless, unknown sounds. At one point,

Lela felt like she'd fallen into a weird, frightening fairytale. All the people around the table were looking at each other, smiling and waving their hands about, laughing every now and then, making speeches and toasts – but what on earth were they saying? Lela listened and wanted to join in, but of course there was no way that she could. Because… really – unbelievably – she didn't understand a word that anyone was saying! It wasn't just that she missed the odd sentence or so: *Lela couldn't understand anything at all in any of the conversations taking place at the table – not a single word!*

In the meantime, the waiters had served roast potatoes, meat, fish and salad. Everyone was helping themselves, piling their plates high with everything they fancied. Lela did the same. Then, they all started talking again. And once again… Lela couldn't understand a word.

It was unbearable!

All of a sudden, Lela had the feeling that she was invisible, voiceless – it was as though she had evaporated into thin air, had ceased to exist, leaving nothing behind but an empty chair.

She felt like she was sitting behind a wall, and only she could see herself. Maybe that was just how it was, and someone had wrapped her up in invisible cotton wool?

'Mum, when are we going to have dessert?' Lela asked, pulling at her mum's dress.

'Later, Lela, you know that!' her mum replied, before turning back to talking to the plump man settled comfortably between her and Lela's father. Lela tried to make out a word

or two of what they were saying but – no. Unfortunately it was all double Dutch to her.

But then – 'Your papa is always so kind, so good-natured.'

Lela suddenly understood something and almost jumped out of her skin.

'Oh yes, my papa is always so kind; he's just wonderful!' she blurted out, looking with approval at the unfamiliar gentleman.

'Shush, Lela! Please don't butt in to our conversation!' said her mum quickly. 'His Excellency is talking about the Pope, not your father!' Then she leant in close and whispered, 'In Spanish, *papa* means *pope*.'

Lela fell into a grumpy silence, turning instead to her plate and taking great care as she searched through her fish for bones. Feeling pretty put out, she tried listening to what the lady in violet on her right was saying. Could it really be that she didn't understand a thing?

'Please ask the elevator to bring me a clean fork, mine has fallen on the floor...' said the lady in violet just then, and Lela laughed. She liked a good joke and people with imagination.

'Mummy, did you hear what she said? The lady wants an elevator to fetch her a clean fork!'

Her mother turned round towards her again. 'Not an elevator, a waiter, Lela! Mrs Edelweiss wanted the *waiter* to pick up her fork and bring her a clean one!' she explained. 'Mixing up words like "elevator" and "waiter" like you did just now is a common mistake if you don't speak English very well.'

Oh! Lela wanted to cry in despair. Big tears started welling up and she fought to hold them back before anyone noticed. Realising she wasn't hungry anymore, Lela pushed her plate away angrily. 'It's all so unfair, so horrible, so silly!' she thought to herself. Lela had definitely heard the lady say "elevator", not "waiter". She'd heard it perfectly clearly.

And she would have said this out loud too, in her fury, if it had been possible... but it wasn't, as Lela was unable to speak even one of the languages the adults were talking to each other in. She started to feel like an empty chair again, spookily invisible and voiceless... Everyone else there could see, hear and understand; it was only Lela who was missing.

It was right then that it happened... Yes, right at that very moment.

Right at that very moment, to her own great surprise, she made a very important promise to herself which would change her life forever.

Right at that very moment, Lela vowed that she... would learn all the languages in the world! Yes, yes, exactly that! She would learn all the languages that there were in the world! At whatever cost! *All of them!*

After a dessert of strawberries and cream, Lela returned home with her mum and dad and started doing just that.

*T*his didn't mean that Lela was going to learn all the languages at once – just a few at first, then lots of them. The more languages she mastered, the easier it would be to get to grips with the next ones. She would start with Latvian, French, Finnish, German, Spanish, Italian, Estonian, Swedish, Slovenian, Maltese, like everyone had been speaking at the party... Yes, these were quite enough to be getting on with. And to begin with, she wouldn't learn every single word – just a few. Every day, more and more words would pop up, and so she would learn more with every passing day.

It happened like this. The day after the party, Lela went straight out to the library and picked up as many dictionaries of different foreign languages as she could lay her hands on. She found ten in total. She put them all in a strong bag and, huffing and puffing, lugged them home. Her mum gave her another, making it eleven. Sitting at her desk, Lela opened the dictionaries and made a neat list of the words she had decided to learn on strips of coloured paper.

The very first phrase she wrote on a strip of paper and learnt in all eleven languages was... GOOD DAY!

In Latvian, it was LABDIEN!

In French, it was BONJOUR!

In Finnish, it was HYVÄÄ PÄIVÄÄ!

In German, it was GUTEN TAG!

In Spanish, it was BUENOS DIAS!

In Italian, it was BUONGIORNO!

In Estonian, it was TERE PÄEVAST!

In Swedish, it was GODDAG!

In Slovenian, it was DOBER DAN!

In Dutch, it was GOEDENDAG!

In Maltese, it was TAIBA JUM!

'That wasn't hard at all!' Lela thought to herself, running through the many different forms of 'good day'. Just then, her beagle Lawrence ran into the room, wagging his tail happily.

'*Buenos dias*, Lawrence!' Lela called out to him.

'Woof, woof!' answered Lawrence in a deep voice, trying to jump on her lap.

'No, not in English, in Spanish please! Please say – *buenos dias*! It's how you say hello in Spanish. Come on now, stop barging into me! But wait, beagles are an English breed of dog, so maybe you'll find *good day* easier to understand!'

'Woof, woof! Woof, woof!' Lawrence's barks revealed a combination of joy and confusion. Still yapping, he tried to lick Lela's face with his warm tongue. She quickly looked up this word, too, in all the dictionaries piled up on her desk.

So, the word FACE...

In Latvian, it was SEJA!
In French, it was VISAGE!
In Finnish, it was KASVOT!
In German, it was GESICHT!
In Spanish, it was CARA!
In Italian, it was VISO!
In Estonian, it was NÄGU!
In Swedish, it was ANSIKTE!
In Slovenian, it was OBRAZ!
In Dutch, it was GEZICHT!
In Maltese, it was WIČČ!

'Lawrence, did you know that you have a speckled *visage*?' said Lela, laughing. He did have a white nose, but the rest of his muzzle around his eyes and his drooping ears was rust-coloured.

Now she had learned these first two words, Lela looked out of the window. Just at that moment, sunbeams began to peek through the intricate branches of their cherry tree, transforming the whole garden into a dazzling, light-filled space, which made her want to run outside – so she did.

*U*sing a piece of chalk she drew squares on the garden path, marking each one with a little number. Then she found a roundish stone and played hopscotch for a while. The stone kept rolling beyond the chalk lines she had drawn, so Lela found another pebble: this one was a little smaller, round and pink. She liked holding it in her hand and every now and then she'd toss it up in the air. This all ended with Lela throwing the pebble high up in the air and catching it and then, taking a powerful swing, lobbing it out – letting it fly wherever it might go.

Tinkle. The sound of breaking glass. Horrified, Lela looked and saw the broken window on her neighbour's conservatory. Shards of broken glass lay on the ground. Lela's heart froze – she didn't know what to do.

Just then, the neighbour's door sprang open and a dark-haired, brown-eyed woman emerged. Lela knew her name was Olga. She had come for a visit from Moscow a week ago. Olga looked at Lela and said something. But Olga didn't speak English. Lela thought she heard words like *stid* and *huliganka*, but she had no idea what they meant. Thankfully, her mum came out just in time and started talking to Olga in the same unfamiliar language. Gradually, the expression on Olga's face changed and she stopped looking so cross. She said goodbye and went back into her house.

'I told her that we would replace the pane of glass. And that you didn't do it on purpose,' Mum explained to Lela. 'You didn't, did you?'

Lela agreed eagerly. Yes, of course, she had absolutely no idea how it could have happened.

'Mum, what language were you both speaking in? I couldn't understand a word.'

'It was Russian,' her mum replied. 'Olga is Russian.'

'Do you have a Russian dictionary as well?'

'I don't, but your dad might – I can have a look,' her mum promised as she opened the front door. Shortly afterwards, Lela found a dictionary with a red cover on her desk. She opened it quickly and was surprised by the strange alphabet all the Russian words were written in. She went and asked her mum for help, and her mum taught her how each and every letter had to be read in this language's alphabet.

So, this time, Lela learnt the word PINK...

In Latvian, it was ROZĀ.
In French, it was ROSE.
In Finnish, it was PINKKI.
In German, it was ROSA.
In Spanish, it was ROSA.
In Italian, it was ROSA.
In Estonian, it was ROOSA.

In Swedish, it was ROSA.

In Slovenian, it was RÓŽEN.

In Dutch, it was ROZE.

In Maltese, it was ROŻA.

In Russian, it was РОЗОВИЙ.

And then she learnt the word STONE...

In Latvian, it was AKMENS.

In French, it was PIERRE.

In Finnish, it was KIVI.

In German, it was STEIN.

In Spanish, it was PIEDRA.

In Italian, it was PIETRA.

In Estonian, it was KIVI.

In Swedish, it was STEN.

In Slovenian, it was KAMEN.

In Dutch, it was STEEN.

In Maltese, it was ĠEBLA.

In Russian, it was КАМЕНЬ.

Now she'd learnt these words, Lela wanted to tackle the next ones immediately but her mum wouldn't let her. She said Lela had to have a little rest. Lela pleaded, saying she didn't want to stop as she hadn't learnt much yet. But Mum gave Lela some money and told her to go and buy herself an ice-cream. When Lela pointed out that she didn't eat sweet things anymore, Mum told her that she really should, as sugar is excellent for brain function. So Lela ran to the nearby shop and bought two ice creams – chocolate for her and an orange one for her mum. She got gluten-free wafers for her dad.

When she got back home, Lela looked up and learnt the word MUM.

In Latvian, it was MAMMA.

In French, it was MAMMAN.

In Finnish, it was ÄITI.

In German, it was MUTTI.

In Spanish, it was MAMA.

In Italian, it was MAMMA.

In Estonian, it was EMME.

In Swedish, it was MAMMA.

In Slovenian, it was MÁMICA.

In Dutch, it was MAMA.

In Maltese, it was MAMÀ.

In Russian, it was MAMA.

When she'd learnt this word, Lela opened her dictionaries again.

This time Lela learnt the word DAD.

In Latvian, it was TĒTIS.

In French, it was PAPA or PÈRE.

In Finnish, it was ISÄ.

In German, it was PAPA.

In Spanish, it was PAPA.

In Italian, it was PAPÀ or BABBO.

In Estonian, it was ISSI.

In Swedish, it was PAPPA.

In Slovenian, it was OČE.

In Dutch, it was PAPA.

In Maltese, it was PAPÀ.

In Russian, it was ПАПА.

'Mummy, did you know that the word "mum" is almost the same in all languages, but "dad" in French is *papa*? Which is the same as in German, Italian, Maltese and Russian?' asked Lela, opening the kitchen door, astonished by her discovery.

'Yes, some words can be similar or even the same from one language to another,' replied her mum, doing the washing up. 'That's why you mixed them up at the dinner table yesterday.'

Lela remembered her mistakes all too well and had no desire to repeat them. Especially not now, when she was studying so hard without anyone telling her to. To try and prove to herself how hardworking she had become, Lela memorised another new word as quick as a flash:

ICE CREAM.

In Latvian, it was SALDĒJUMS!

In French, it was GLACE!

In Finnish, it was JÄÄTELO !

In German, it was EIS!

In Spanish, it was HELADO!

In Italian, it was GELATO!

In Estonian, it was JÄÄTIS!

In Swedish, it was GLASS!

In Slovenian, it was SLADOLÉD!

In Dutch, it was IJS!

In Maltese, it was ĠELAT!

In Russian, it was МОРОЖЕНОЕ!

'Lela, did you bring back any change from the shop?' asked her mum suddenly, startling her.

'Yes,' Lela replied, remembering that she had. 'I'll give it back to you…'

'No, you can put it in your money box,' her mum replied. Lela was delighted – she'd been saving for a couple of weeks now to buy some magic pencils. They were special because they changed colour on the paper.

After putting the remaining coins into her money box, Lela looked up and learnt the word MONEY.

In Latvian, it was NAUDA.

In French, it was ARGENT.

In Finnish, it was RAHA.

In German, it was GELD.

In Spanish, it was DINERO.

In Italian, it was SOLDI.

In Estonian, it was RAHA.

In Swedish, it was PENGAR.

In Slovenian, it was DENÁR.

In Dutch, it was GELD.

In Maltese, it was FLUS.

In Russian, it was ДЕНЬГИ.

Hello, my child! Aren't you going to come and say hello to me?' The door opened unexpectedly and who should be there but Grandma, smiling at her.

'Grandma!' Lela exclaimed happily, and flung herself at a slim, delicate figure in a pearl-grey dress with pink flowers on it and neatly-done hair covered by a light-coloured straw hat. Lela's grandma lived at the other end of the city in a big beautiful house surrounded by hollyhocks, honeysuckle and sugarplums. Grandma herself was named after a flower, or to be precise after a spring flower – Primrose. Lela knew that her grandmother had been named after her own mother, who had been named for the first flower of spring.

'When did you get here?' asked Lela, genuinely surprised. 'I didn't hear you arrive!'

'Your mother is correct: you seem to have got completely carried away,' said Grandma, glancing at Lela's desk strewn with a vast quantity of dictionaries and colourful notes.

'I'm studying words in different languages!' Lela explained. 'I'm going to learn all the languages in the world! Do you think I can do it?'

'You? Well of course! Even if it takes you a lifetime!' Grandma Primrose agreed. 'But every so often, do you think

you could try to put all this to one side and take your head out of these books? Have a rest and stop thinking about all this. Be a bit flighty – like a dragonfly or a butterfly. Your head might explode otherwise.'

'Like a dragonfly?' Lela asked and shook her head. 'No, Grandma, I can't be like that right now... but I wouldn't mind being a little bird!'

'Well, I won't disturb you any further,' Grandma said, smiling, and she closed the door behind her.

Lela immediately learnt the word CHILD.

In Latvian, it was BĒRNS.

In French, it was ENFANT.

In Finnish, it was LAPSI.

In German, it was KIND.

In Spanish, it was NIÑO.

In Italian, it was BAMBINO.

In Estonian, it was LAPS.

In Swedish, it was BARN.

In Slovenian, it was OTRÒK.

In Dutch, it was KIND.

In Maltese, it was TFAL (CHILDREN),
TIFEL (A BOY), TIFLA (A GIRL).

In Russian, it was РЕБЁНОК.

Then she learnt the word HAT.

In Latvian, it was CEPURE.

In French, it was CHAPEAU.

In Finnish, it was HATTU.

In German, it was HUT.

In Spanish, it was SOMBRERO.

In Italian, it was CAPELLO.

In Estonian, it was MÜTS

In Swedish, it was HATT.

In Slovenian, it was ČÉPICA.

In Dutch, it was HOED.

In Maltese, it was KAPPELL.

In Russian, it was ШАПКА.

There was a light knock on the door and Grandma was there again.

'I'm sorry to bother you again, but what kind of bird would you like to be?' she asked.

'What?' Lela had already forgotten what they had just been talking about. 'Oh! I would like to be... a swallow! Yes, because they're such fast flyers!'

When her grandma had left, Lela found and learnt the word BUTTERFLY.

In Latvian, it was TAURENIS.

In French, it was PAPILLON.

In Finnish, it was PERHONEN.

In German, it was SCHMETTERLING.

In Spanish, it was MARIPOSA.

In Italian, it was FARFALLA.

In Estonian, it was LIBLIKAS.

In Swedish, it was FJÄRIL.

In Slovenian, it was MÉTULJ.

In Dutch, it was VLINDER.

In Maltese, it was FARFETT.

In Russian, it was БАБОЧКА.

'*Far-fett*,' Lela repeated to herself as the door sprang open and her mum appeared in the doorway.

'Lela, your grandma is worrying about how much you're studying. Have you fed Jirki today?' her mum asked.

'Oh! I'll do it straight away,' Lela leapt to her feet and rushed to the aquarium that stood in the corner of her room. Her goldfish, Jirki, was gliding gracefully through the bubbles and colourful water plants. He was a very special fish, because her dad had given him to Lela for her birthday. And he hadn't just bought the fish at a pet shop – he had brought him back from Finland, frozen in a glossy slab of ice. Her mum hadn't believed that the fish could survive, but the ice had melted and he'd come back to life. This was why he had a Finnish name – he came from Finland! Jirki was the name of the Finnish ambassador, a good friend of her father's. Lela thought that the name suited her fish perfectly. But now… didn't he look a little sad and hungry?

'I'm sorry Jirki, I was studying and I forgot all about you,' Lela said, pouring a more-generous-than-usual serving of fish food into the aquarium.

After watching the fish for a while, opening his lips to eat the food and gliding from side to side, Lela went back to her desk.

This time, she learnt the word WATER.

In Latvian, it was ŪDENS.

In French, it was EAU.

In Finnish, it was VESI.

In German, it was WASSER.

In Spanish, it was AGUA.

In Italian, it was ACQUA.

In Estonian, it was VESI.

In Swedish, it was VATTEN.

In Slovenian, it was VŎDA.

In Dutch, it was WATER.

In Maltese, it was ILMA.

In Russian, it was ВОДА.

And she also learnt the word FISH.

In Latvian, it was ZIVS.

In French, it was POISSON.

In Finnish, it was KALA.

In German, it was FISCH.

In Spanish, it was PEZ.

In Italian, it was PESCE.

In Estonian, it was KALA.

In Swedish, it was FISK.

In Slovenian, it was RÍBA.

In Dutch, it was VIS.

In Maltese, it was ĦUTA.

In Russian, it was РЫБА.

'The little fish!' Lela exclaimed, remembering the shape that Līga, her Sunday school teacher, had recently shown them how to fold from a sheet of paper – they were really cute, especially when you drew in some scales and fins, eyes and a mouth.

'I'll give it a try!' Lela decided, picking up a square piece of paper and starting to fold.

First, she folded the piece of paper crosswise in a diagonal to make a triangle, and then she unfolded it again. Then she did the same crosswise in the other direction. This made it easy to see the exact centre of the paper: the dot where the two lines crossed.

Then she took one corner and folded it in towards the centre. She then did the same with the opposite corner.

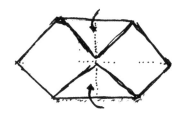

Then Lela folded the square in half diagonally, making a shape a bit like a boat.

She started folding from the left, folding the lower corner of the boat A with the central point V. She did the same with the left corner B then the upper left corner, C.

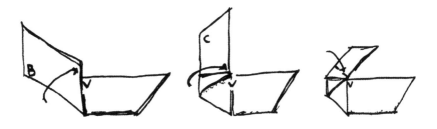

She then spun the fish-to-be around and repeated the folding procedure from the left: folding the lower corner up to central point V, before repeating the same action with both the middle and upper corner.

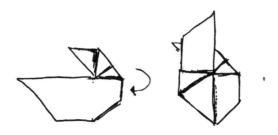

Now she only had to fold over the corners of the tail or fins and she had made a fish.

'I did it!' Lela shouted joyfully, putting the folded fish into the basket to join the others.

She thought for a while and then taught herself the word BUBBLE.

In Latvian, it was BURBULIS.

In French, it was BULLE.

In Finnish, it was KUPLA.

In German, it was BLASE.

In Spanish, it was BURBUJA.

In Italian, it was BOLLA.

In Estonian, it was MULL.

In Swedish, it was BUBBLA.

In Slovenian, it was MEHÚRČEK.

In Dutch, it was BUBBEL.

In Maltese, it was BUŻŻIEQA.

In Russian, it was ПУЗЫРЬ.

Then she taught herself the word SAD.

In Latvian, it was BĒDĪGS.

In French, it was TRISTE.

In Finnish, it was SURULLINEN.

In German, it was TRAURIG.

In Spanish, it was TRISTE.

In Italian, it was TRISTE.

In Estonian, it was KURB.

In Swedish, it was LEDSEN.

In Slovenian, it was ŽÁLOSTEN.

In Dutch, it was VERDRIETIG.

In Maltese, it was IMDEJJAQ.

In Russian, it was ПЕЧАЛЪНЫЙ.

Once she had learnt these words, Lela wanted to memorise some more, but then, all of a sudden, something unexpected happened. Without warning, all the new words started leaping and fluttering into Lela's head like colourful balls. There was a red bead *dober dan* and a yellow *steen*. There was a green *issi* and a blue *pengar*. A pink *lapsi* and a white *kappell* too... Meanwhile Lawrence, yapping noisily, had popped up by her side again. Every now and then, the dog looked pointedly at the peg where his lead hung and his whining became more insistent.

'All right, let's go! It's time for a break!' Lela called to Lawrence, snatching up his lead. The dog was so excited that he nearly made a puddle on the floor! Once they were outside, he ran along the pavement impatiently, sniffing all around him.

On their walk, Lawrence met three other dogs and a couple of cats. And several crows, which he barked loudly and furiously at. He also cocked his leg against a lamppost, leaving a message for other dogs along Violet Lane, Plumtree Lane and Kings Avenue. Lela hoped his message wouldn't go unread, as she noticed the dark clouds overhead and the first raindrops started to fall. Lela saw several earthworms that had sneaked out of the ground to enjoy the rain.

When they got back home, Lela felt a bit tired. But after a short rest, she got straight back to studying new words.

This time, Lela learnt the word LETTER.

In Latvian, it was VĒSTULE.

In French, it was LETTRE.

In Finnish, it was KIRJE.

In German, it was BRIEF.

In Spanish, it was CARTA.

In Italian, it was LETTERA.

In Estonian, it was KIRI.

In Swedish, it was BREV.

In Slovenian, it was PISMO.

In Dutch, it was BRIEF.

In Maltese, it was ITTRA.

In Russian, it was ПИСМО.

And she learnt the word DOG too:

In Latvian, it was SUNS.

In French, it was CHIEN.

In Finnish, it was KOIRA.

In German, it was HUND.

In Spanish, it was PERRO.

In Italian, it was CANE.

In Estonian, it was KOER.

In Swedish, it was HUND.

In Slovenian, it was PES.

In Dutch, it was HOND.

In Maltese, it was KELB.

In Russian, it was СОБАКА.

All of a sudden, Lela remembered that she had some homework to do for the next day. The teacher had asked them to draw a picture of a friend. As she looked for some colouring pencils and paper, Lela decided to draw a dog. Her dog of course – Lawrence the beagle.

'He looks a bit lonely all on his own,' Lela decided, examining the drawing once she'd finished. So, next to Lawrence, she added a black crow.

On the scrap of paper she wrote down what the word CROW was in other languages:

In Latvian, it was VĀRNA.

In French, it was CORNEILLE.

In Finnish, it was VARIS.

In German, it was KRÄHE.

In Spanish, it was CUERVO

In Italian, it was CORNACCHIA

In Estonian, it was VARES.

In Swedish, it was KRÅKA.

In Slovenian, it was VRÁNA.

In Dutch, it was KRAAI.

In Maltese, it was ĊAWLA.

In Russian, it was ВОРОНА.

And she also learnt the word EARTHWORM.

In Latvian, it was SLIEKA.

In French, it was VER DE TERRE.

In Finnish, it was KASTEMATO.

In German, it was REGENWURM.

In Spanish, it was GUSANO.

In Italian, it was LOMBRICO.

In Estonian, it was VIHMAUSS.

In Swedish, it was DAGGMASK.

In Slovenian, it was DEŽÉVNIK.

In Dutch, it was REGENWORM.

In Maltese, it was ĦANEX.

In Russian, it was ДОЖДЕВОЙ ЧЕРВЬ.

Just then, Lela gave a loud sneeze: 'ATCHOO!' The sneeze was so loud that it bunged up her ears.

'Bless you!' someone called out. The door immediately sprang open and her mum poked her head round the door. 'Would you like some blackcurrant juice or a lemon squash? Or a milkshake, maybe?'

'Thank you! I'd like a milkshake, please,' Lela said. 'And I'm fine! Just sneezing a bit.'

And straight away she looked up and learnt a new word – SNEEZE.

In Latvian, it was ŠĶAVAS.

In French, it was ÉTERNUEMENT.

In Finnish, it was AIVASTUS.

In German, it was NIESEN.

In Spanish, it was ESTORNUDO.

In Italian, it was STARNUTO.

In Estonian, it was AEVASTUS.

In Swedish, it was NYSNIG.

In Slovenian, it was KÍHANJE.

In Dutch, it was NIEZEN.

In Maltese, it was GĦATSA.

In Russian, it was ЧИХАНЬЕ.

Before looking up any more words, Lela went down to the kitchen to enjoy the delicious milkshake her mum had made with strawberries, banana, milk and ice cream. And a pinch of vanilla sugar. Lela sat at her desk, slurping the refreshing drink through a sky blue straw, and felt so inspired that she learnt the word MILK.

In Latvian, it was PIENS.

In French, it was LAIT.

In Finnish, it was MAITO.

In German, it was MILCH.

In Spanish, it was LECHE.

In Italian, it was LETTE.

In Estonian, it was PIIM.

In Swedish, it was MJÖLK.

In Slovenian, it was MLÉKO.

In Dutch, it was MELK.

In Maltese, it was ĦALIB.

In Russian, it was МОЛОКО.

She also learnt the word STRAWBERRY.

In Latvian, it was ZEMENE.

In French, it was FRAISE.

In Finnish, it was MANSIKKA.

In German, it was ERDBEERE.

In Spanish, it was FRESA.

In Italian, it was FRAGOLA.

In Estonian, it was MAASIKAS.

In Swedish, it was JORDGUBBAR.

In Slovenian, it was RDEČA JÁGODA.

In Dutch, it was AARDBEI.

In Maltese, it was FRAWLA.

In Russian, it was КЛУБНИКА.

*W*hen *she had memorised* these words, Lela finally felt worn out and she decided to take a break. She thought she'd call her friend Clara. Clara had black curly hair that looked like whirly snakes and she wore glasses. She loved yoghurt mixed with dried banana chips with sugar on top – Lela couldn't understand how anyone could like such a combination. Just as Lela was picking her phone up from the shelf, it rang. She looked at the screen and it was...

'Clara! Amazing! Thanks for calling! Guess what I'm doing?' Lela told her friend all about everything she'd learnt that day and how many words in different languages she had memorised, and asked if Clara wanted to try it too. Clara was surprised and excited. She said she definitely wanted to study all the languages in the world, just like Lela. She just had to pop to the shopping centre with her dad first. And also... a documentary about dolphins was about to start on TV. Clara said she really wanted to watch it, as dolphins were so beautiful and she found them absolutely fascinating! Maybe she would start tomorrow? But no, she couldn't, she was going to Auntie Lusianna's for lunch with her family.

'Which words did you learn?' Clara asked, and Lela told her everything in great detail.

'And can you still remember them all?' Clara was amazed, her voice a little envious. 'Hmm, maybe I'll try to stay home tomorrow and study like you,' she added. 'And then... and then...' Clara burst out laughing. Lela had no idea why.

'What? What are you laughing about?' she asked.

'Then... then we'll learn... some other words, too. Get what I mean?' her friend answered, bursting into a fit of giggles.

'What kind of words?' Lela still didn't get it.

'Hmm, well, you know!' Clara gave another snort of laughter and whispered some of the words she was thinking of into the phone. Now both of them were giggling.

'Aren't these words rude?' Lela asked.

'Words are there to be used!' Clara said and hung up.

*J*ust then, Lela heard an odd noise outside, somewhere near their house – like something huge and impossible to grasp was coming near. Lela rushed over to the window and looked outside... A hot air balloon! It was enormous! The immense dome looked rather like an orange basketball and the wondrous thing was floating just above the potato field next to their garden, a few inches from the ground. She couldn't believe her eyes! Astonished, Lela dashed out of the room, bumping into her mum and grandma in the doorway as they also went out to look at the amazing aircraft. All three of them stared at the bright hot air balloon and woven flying basket still hovering in the air – flames of fire from the burner, operated by the pilot, kept it bobbing just above the ground. The pilot was short, with cropped dark hair and tightly-fitting goggles on his nose. He had a fine pair of binoculars hanging by a leather cord around his neck. Lela imagined that he must be able to see far, far away with them.

'Is your name Lela?' the pilot asked, removing his goggles to reveal bright blue eyes.

'Yes, that's me,' Lela answered, embarrassed.

'Then climb in, please!' the pilot smiled, indicating the rope ladder thrown over the side of the basket.

'Can I?' Lela asked incredulously, looking at Mum and Grandma.

'Of course! We'll wait here for you on the ground,' her mum promised, waving Lela off.

'This is precisely what I meant when I told you to be more flighty. Don't you remember?' Grandma asked.

'Oh, I didn't realise you meant it so literally!' Lela exclaimed and hugged her Grandma.

'Words can be literal, too,' Grandma Primrose added, wisely.

'Brilliant!' Lela agreed. 'I just need to go and get something. I'll nip back indoors a second...'

'If you're planning on carting a dictionary along, forget it. For half an hour, at least!' Mum told Lela. Lela knew she was right. It would be almost impossible to write while travelling in a hot air balloon, and she certainly wouldn't have time to study.

Then whoosh, Lela was flying skywards in a hot air balloon! She felt just as Grandma had said she should earlier – like a dragonfly or a butterfly. It was amazing! She heard a loud hissing as the flames heated the air, lifting the balloon upwards. Lela peeped tentatively over the edge of the basket. From above, everything looked much smaller and neater. The houses looked like toys, and so did the trees and bushes. The river and its side streams looked like a tangled blue ribbon.

'Would you like to take a look through my binoculars?' the pilot unexpectedly offered Lela.

Goodness, now everything seemed so incredibly close! Just as she had imagined! She felt she could almost touch the pinecones on the tops of the fir trees! The registration plates on the cars, too! What a mighty pair of binoculars! All of a sudden, Lela's gaze focused on a little pink spot, also on the move. She wasn't sure she could believe her eyes! She quickly swung the binoculars to follow the movement, but the balloon had already flown a good way ahead. 'I must have imagined it,' Lela told herself, giving the binoculars back to their owner.

'What if a strong wind gets up?' she thought suddenly. 'What if it rips the hot air balloon off the basket or capsizes it? And how do we know where we are flying? What if the wind carries us to America or India?'

Lela, worried, looked at the pilot and saw him smiling.

'Don't worry, Lela,' the pilot said, having guessed what was worrying her. 'I have a map that keeps me from getting lost, look!' And he showed Lela a colourful drawing, the likes of which Lela had never seen before. 'Look, meadows and forests are marked here, and here's the river and here are the most important buildings in the city!'

At first, Lela couldn't make sense of it, but, taking a closer look, everything became clear. She calmed down.

'What was that building with the tall chimney that we flew over a while ago?' Lela was curious.

'That? That was the old dairy. Want one?' the pilot asked, offering Lela a pack of sour candies.

'Yes, please!' Lela said, helping herself. Open-mouthed in wonder, she continued staring at the wonderful scene below.

'Has this hot air balloon got a name?' she wanted to know.

'*Orange Dream!*'

That was when it happened. The wind dropped and the air became completely still but then, all of a sudden, a scrap of paper flew in front of Lela's face out of nowhere. It fluttered in the air like it was asking the girl to take it. And Lela did just that. She stretched her arm through the ropes attached to the basket and quickly snatched the scrap of paper. Sentences in a foreign language were written on it, maybe even in several languages. There was a photo attached, too. Lela turned to the pilot but he just shook his head.

'Sorry, but I don't understand what's written there,' the pilot confessed.

Lela took a closer look at the text, not entirely sure of herself. She had studied so hard today. Maybe she could at least take a guess at what it meant?

And she could. Lela understood some words quite well, others not so well but the sense of the message was clear. Especially when she looked at the photo attached. So the note, that looked a little like a letter or a flyer, said this:

Hello!
My name is Mary Jane and I'm sad as my rabbit, called --- has gone missing...
Distinguishing features: white all over with a black face, wearing a pink waistcoat, he likes earthworms and ice cream with strawberries. Please help me!!!!!! Whoever

finds him is kindly requested to report in person to 3A, Sunshine Street.

The text was a little blurred in places and hard to read and all the punctuation had practically faded but its meaning was clear. Lela noticed that several words beneath the flyer were in other foreign languages. Lela recognized English, French, German and Swedish. She was a little perplexed at the rabbit apparently having a fondness for earthworms. Even so, there was no doubt about it – and less so as she stared at the colour photo. Despite being quite tiny, she could make out a white rabbit in a pink waistcoat quite clearly, squatting amongst purple lavender bushes. His nose was smattered with black freckles.

'When are we going to fly back home?' Lela asked the pilot.

'Do you really want to turn back already?' he asked.

'Yes, please, as soon as possible!' Lela replied, anxiously. 'We have to rescue someone!'

'Rescue?' the pilot repeated, shaking his head in disbelief.

'He is tiny and totally lost!' Lela replied, true despair in her voice.

The pilot didn't know what to make of it.

A few moments later Lela's own street, house and flourishing potato field came back into view. From above, it looked like a blue and green square. Lela watched wide-eyed as the pilot, with blasts of leaping flames, directed the balloon straight to the very centre of the field and, after a couple of bumps of the basket, landed right on it. Mum and Grandma stood at the edge of the field, waving at Lela. Her dad, too, was back from the Ministry, with Lawrence leaping and barking noisily at his feet.

'Congratulations, Lela!' the pilot said when they had landed. 'You shall now be known Countess Lela von Bluepotatoflower!'

Lela looked at him in astonishment.

'It's a tradition – everyone is given a title in honour of the place they land after their first flight in a hot air balloon,' explained the pilot of the Orange Dream.

'I had no idea I had such a courageous daughter,' her father announced proudly as he joined them.

'Courageous and hard-working!' her grandma and mum added.

'Mum! Dad!' Lela interrupted her parents. 'We have to hurry! I've just received a letter! Lawrence, will you stop that, please!' she shouted at the dog who was pawing her trousers joyfully with dirty feet.

'Letter? What letter?' Mum wondered.

'The wind brought it to me while I was flying in the hot air balloon!' she said, showing them the peculiar flyer.

Having read the note, her dad looked at her in astonishment, asking 'Lela, do you understand what it says? It says that ...'

'Yes, I do!' Lela confirmed eagerly. 'I understand it all too well! I actually saw him! Lawrence, cut it out!'

'What did you see?' her dad asked.

'The rabbit!' Lela replied. 'Dad, will you take me to the old dairy? The pilot gave me his binoculars and I saw everything as clear as can be! And the rabbit was real, take my word for it!'

'But Lela…' her dad was at a loss. 'This is no ordinary letter. Do you see what's written here? It says the rabbit is wearing… a waistcoat!'

'Yes, a pink one! That's why I noticed him, I couldn't believe my eyes!' Lela was already racing towards the garage. Her mum and dad had no option but to follow – only Grandma stayed at home.

Lela was so over-excited that she wriggled impatiently in her car seat. When the car stopped, she was the first to leap out. Yes, this was the building she had seen through the binoculars. Look, there was the red brick chimney! And look, there was the grove of young fir trees where, from high above in the balloon, Lela had seen something that at first she could hardly believe was true – a white rabbit in a little pink waistcoat. Lela slowed down, as she didn't want to frighten the rabbit off. She looked carefully all around but there was nothing pink to be seen. Had she imagined it all? But what about the flyer and photo? She certainly hadn't made them up – the wind had blown the peculiar piece of paper right into her hands!

'So where is this rabbit of yours?' Mum asked, coming up to Lela, her voice betraying the fact that she didn't really believe in the rabbit at all.

'He must be round here somewhere,' Lela answered, her eyes still searching for him under the trees. 'He must have something still to do here…'

Saying this, Lela made a pair of binoculars with her curled-up hands and squatted down, looking through them. Turning to the right, she spied the trousers of her dad's dark grey suit; turning to the left, her mum's red and black checked skirt.

'Perhaps it wasn't a rabbit after all?' Her dad was more direct.

Lela wanted to disagree but – there was no rabbit to be seen. Letting out a sad sigh, Lela turned her hand-binoculars towards the colourful tulip bed not far from the young fir trees. Oh! What was that moving there? In a flash, Lela darted to the flowerbed. There he was – small, white and fluffy! Just his nose was speckled black.

'Don't be scared, little rabbit!' Lela said soothingly, squatting down. She stretched out her hands and... the little rabbit leapt straight into her arms! It was as if he had been waiting impatiently for her all along! It was just then that her mum and dad came rushing to her side.

'What did I tell you!?' Lela crowed, showing them the little creature.

'A little waistcoat, indeed! All he needs is some trousers!' her mum exclaimed. 'Isn't he adorable!'

They drove to 3A, Sunshine Street, the address written on the flyer. It was a two-storey, solid-looking wooden building surrounded by a high wooden fence.

'How on earth could he have got out of here?' Dad wondered, ringing the bell at the gate.

It took a while for anyone to open the gate, and when someone did Lela was disappointed. She had imagined the Mary Jane on the flyer to be a girl of about her own age, so she was surprised to see a lady as old as Grandma Primrose. As the woman saw the rabbit in Lela's hands, she burst into a smile.

'Pink, you naughty boy! Where have you been? And how did they find you?' she said, reaching out for her rabbit. The rabbit did another of his astounding leaps, now familiar to Lela, and in one sleek, springy move jumped straight into his owner's arms.

'Pink?' her mum asked. 'That's a name I haven't heard before!'

'Yes, Pink,' the rabbit's owner confirmed. 'I also have Black, Red and Green. They are all as white as snowballs with just their little faces speckled black, all practically identical!

So I don't get them mixed them up, I dress them in different coloured waistcoats! Thank you very much for bringing him home! Thank you from the bottom of my heart! Someone left the gate open, the one you just came through, and he got out. But please, do come in! I'll show you the other rabbits! My name is Mary Jane Dannenberg.'

Lela, her mum and her dad were soon looking at them, each as colourful as Easter eggs. All four rabbits hopped about on the kitchen floor – Lela couldn't take her eyes off their cheerful lolloping. Lela told the story once more to the kind rabbit owner, of how she had spied Pink through binoculars

whilst flying in a hot air balloon and how the wind had blown the flyer straight into her hands.

'Yes, why did you write it in different languages?' her dad wanted to know.

'I was so desperate, I thought it might improve my chances,' the old lady confessed. 'I was hoping for a miracle and for Pink to be found! It just came out like that!' She urged Lela and her parents to help themselves to hot chocolate and yet another slice of her homemade currant cake.

'Can you really speak all those languages?' Lela's mum was filled with admiration. 'You wrote in German as well as French and Swedish! In all those languages!'

'I used to be able to speak them all quite well,' Mary Jane nodded. 'Now I've forgotten a lot of things. Thank goodness I still have the dictionaries that belonged to my late husband – I had to check a few words when I wrote the flyer,' she explained.

'But how did you distribute the flyers, if you don't mind my asking?' Lela's dad asked.

Mary Jane blushed.

'I scattered them from the top of the tower!' she explained. 'The church tower! I didn't think there was much point sticking them to lampposts, and I wouldn't have had the energy for that anyway. I knew that at six o'clock every morning Jim goes up to ring the bells for morning mass, so I crept up behind him, unnoticed. While he was ringing the bells, I scattered the flyers into the wind – they tore away like a snowstorm!'

'But... is it true that Pink eats ice cream and earthworms?' Lela suddenly recalled.

'Earthworms? What nonsense!' The rabbit's owner sounded quite indignant.

'But that's what it says here!' said Lela, timidly stretching out the flyer.

Mary Jane glanced at it and laughed.

'No, my dear! You've got it wrong! What is says is that you'll get an ice cream as a reward, to warm your heart. *Heart warm*, not *earthworm*!'

'No need for that!' Lela's mum said firmly. 'We were happy to help. No reward needed.'

'See it as doing each other a good turn,' Mary Jane countered. 'And I'm delighted that not all children these days are spoilt and that some still believe in little rabbits with pink waistcoats. So please, do take the ice cream I'd like to give you on your way out.'

'Well, if Pink's owner insists, I'll let you have a second ice cream today,' Mum whispered to Lela.

Lela's mum had got it all wrong, however, as on their way out Mary Jane Dannenberg handed them not one ice cream, but a whole box filled to the brim with ice creams!

'You can't imagine that Pink is worth just one measly ice cream cone, can you?' Mary Jane said when Lela's mum started to make a fuss.

*B*ack at home Lela rushed to her room. She wanted to learn even more new words before she went to bed. Her adventure with the rabbit had confirmed that Lela was on the right path. Just one day earlier and she would hardly have understood anything on that flyer, and instead she had understood nearly everything Mary Jane had written. Except for the part about earthworms, of course.

This time, she learnt the word SWEETS:

In Latvian, it was CANDY.

In French, it was BONBON.

In Finnish, it was KARKKI.

In German, it was BONBON.

In Spanish, it was CARAMELO.

In Italian, it was CARAMELLA.

In Estonian, it was KOMM.

In Swedish, it was GODIS.

In Slovenian, it was SLADKÓRČEK.

In Dutch, it was SNOEP.

In Maltese, it was ĦELWA.

In Russian, it was КОНФЕТА.

And she learnt the word BALL

In Latvian, it was BUMBA.

In French, it was BALLE.

In Finnish, it was PALLO.

In German, it was BALL.

48

In Spanish, it was PELOTA.

In Italian, it was PALLA.

In Estonian, it was PALL.

In Swedish, it was BOLL.

In Slovenian, it was ŽOGA.

In Dutch, it was BAL.

In Maltese, it BALLUN.

In Russian, it was МЯЧ.

Just then, Lela remembered the map the hot air balloon pilot had shown her and decided to draw her own. Her map might not have been exactly spot on, but she remembered a lot. Lela would be able to show it to Clara when she told her about her flight! Grabbing a sheet of paper and colouring pencils, she was completely absorbed in her drawing. When she had finished, the following were all clearly marked:

Lela's House (1), the next door neighbour's house (the one with the broken porch window) (2), the local church where Mary Jane Dannenberg had scattered the flyers about her missing rabbit (3), the pharmacy next door (4), the market square (5), the bridge across the winding river (6) and, of course, the old dairy (7).

Straight away she also learnt the word MAP:

In Latvian, it was KARTE.

In French, it was PLAN.

In Finnish, it was KARTTA.

In German, it was KARTE.

In Spanish, it was MAPA.

In Italian, it was MAPPA.

In Estonian, it was KAART.

In Swedish, it was KARTA.

In Slovenian, it was ZEMLJEVID.

In Dutch, it was KAART.

In Maltese, it was MAPPA.

In Russian, it was KAPTA.

And, just to be on the safe side, she also learnt the word HELP!

In Latvian, it was PALĪGĀ!

In French, it was À L'AIDE!

In Finnish, it was APUA!

In German, it was HILFE!

In Spanish, it was AYUDA!

In Italian, it was AIUTA!

In Estonian, it was APPI!

In Swedish, it was HJÄLP!

In Slovenian, it was NA POMÓČ!

In Dutch, it was HELP!

In Maltese, it was AJJUT!

In Russian, it was НА ПОМОЩЪ!

Going over to the door, Lela suddenly shouted, '*Hjälp! Hjälp!*' (the Swedish word for 'help'!) at the top of her voice. The door slammed open almost immediately and her dad, mum and grandma came running into her room.

'Whatever is the matter?!' they asked, speaking over each other and all looking so worried that Lela felt embarrassed.

'Sorry! I was only testing to see if I had the right word. Seems I have!'

When she was alone once more in her room,

she learnt the word MIRACLE.

In Latvian, it was BRĪNUMS.
In French, it was MIRACLE.
In Finnish, it was IHME.
In German, it was WUNDER.
In Spanish, it was MILAGRO.
In Italian, it was MIRACOLO.
In Estonian, it was IME.
In Swedish, it was MIRAKEL.
In Slovenian, it was ČÚDEŽ.
In Dutch, it was WONDER.
In Maltese, it was MIRAKLU.
In Russian, it was ЧУДО.

Having spent a while memorising these words, Lela made faces at herself in the mirror (she tried to touch the end of her nose with her tongue, but it was easier said than done). Suddenly, her phone rang. It was Clara ringing her, so late at night!

'It looks like we're not going to visit my aunt tomorrow after all!' she told Lela. 'I'll come round to see you and we can study together! It'll be fun, won't it?'

'Yes, it will!' Lela agreed wholeheartedly, before going on to tell her all about her adventure in the hot air balloon, with the binoculars and the rabbit.

'You went flying through the air and saw a little rabbit in a pink waistcoat? You must be telling fibs! All he needed was a little pair of trousers!' Clara exclaimed, saying almost the same as Lela's mum.

Lela realised there was no point arguing. Tomorrow, when she showed Clara her map and the photo her dad had taken of her and Pink, there would be no more talk of trousers.

'Did you learn a lot of words today?' Clara wanted to know.

Lela read them all out. It was quite a long list!

'Well done, Lela!' congratulated Clara. 'Although you've forgotten some of the most important ones...'

'Which ones?' asked Lela.

'You know exactly which! Tell me those ones and we'll memorise them together!' her friend said, all in one breath.

And so they did. They learnt the last words for that evening together.

The first word was FART.

In Latvian, it was PURKŠĶIS.

In French, it was PET.

In Finnish, it was PIERU.

In German, it was PUPSEN.

In Spanish, it was PEDO.

In Italian, it was SCOREGGIA

In Estonian, it was PEER.

In Swedish, it was PRUTT.

In Slovenian, it was PŘDEC.

In Dutch, it was SCHEET.

In Maltese, it was BASSA.

In Russian, it was БЗД

And then the girls learnt the word POO just in case it came in handy:

In Latvian, it was KAKA.

In French, it was CACA.

In Finnish, it was PASKA.

In German, it was KAKA.

In Spanish, it was CACA.

In Italian, it was POPÒ or CACCA.

In Estonian, it was KAKA.

In Swedish, it was BAJS.

In Slovenian, it was DREK.

In Dutch, it was POEP.

In Maltese, it was KOKÒ.

In Russian, it was КАКАШКА.

'I love how expressive these words are, they sound great!' Clara said after they'd said them loudly and clearly several times over. Lela's dad had told her this was the best way to memorise them.

'I think I prefer these words to all the others ...' Clara was laughing again.

'Don't be silly!' Lela told her friend. 'You never know which word might come in handy.' And she told her friend about how frightened she had been up in the balloon and how she had learned the word 'help' as soon as she landed.

'Trust me, in an emergency, "help!" is far more useful than any other word we've just learnt. All the same, next time Rudolph from the class next door pulls your hair and call you "Curly locks" you'll be able to call him a stinky *pupsen* or a right *paska*.'

Just then, Lela's mum came into the bedroom and was shocked to hear Lela using such language. In turn, Lela was surprised at her mum's astonishment. 'Words are there to be used,' she said. 'Everyone goes to the toilet at least once a day (unless they're constipated) and the person who has never farted has yet to be born.'

'You know, Mum, I feel so much wiser than I was this morning, before I learned all these new words,' said Lela. 'Now I know that cats meow because they're cats, mice squeak because they're made that way, dogs bark because they have to and people study and learn more languages because they're human. Not cats or dogs or mice. And tomorrow morning, I'll carry on learning all the other languages in the world!'

THE END

WHO MADE
THIS BOOK?

About the author

Ieva Flamingo (the pen name of Ieva Samauska) is one of the most prolific Latvian children's authors writing today. She was a journalist at various newspapers and magazines, but ten years ago she became a full-time children's writer.

To date she has published 23 books, of poems, stories, fairy tales with various different publishers. She won the Pastariņš Prize for Latvian Children's Literature in 2015 and her books have been nominated for the International Jānis Baltvilks Baltic Sea Region Award several times.

Her first collection of lyrical poems, *Kā uzburt sniegu /How to conjure up snow* (liels un mazs, 2006), was adapted for the Latvian National Theatre in 2007.

Ieva lives in Saldus, a small town in Latvia, with her family, three cats and a white dog Alba.

AN INTERVIEW WITH IEVA

When did you start writing stories?

When I was a child, I liked to look at nature and write my observations down afterwards. For example, once I remember taking a walk in a forest with my parents and brother. We heard some strange sounds, and it turned out to be little rabbit that had fallen into a trap.

We rescued him and I wrote a story: 'The Unhappy Bunny'. This was my first publication in a newspaper, which made me very happy.

Do you remember your very first story?

I wrote my first real story when I was studying journalism. It was around the time of revolution in Latvia, when Latvia was geting its independence back from Russia.

Back then, you could only buy certain groceries and chocolate with special vouchers. I didn't like this situation and I started to write (on a typewriter, because we didn't have computers yet) my first story for children: 'The Great Chocolate Rescue'. This was about a country named Vatlia, its president and his hundred advisers.

In this story, everyone suffers from a strange disease, like a syndrome of tastebud confusion. This means that all they want to eat is sweets, and nothing else. That's why they have banned sweets in the whole country. A little girl called Kate and her friends try to solve this situation.

Did you enjoy studying languages at school?

At school we were taught Russian. It was mandatory and we had many lessons a week. Later on we were taught English. Unfortunately these language lessons were still in their early stages, so they weren't as good as they are now at my daughter's school.

I remember a lot of grammar and the vocabulary from different topics, but without hearing the language or the correct pronunciations and without using it every day – it wasn't easy. Maybe this is one of the reasons I wrote this book – searching for the joy of knowing languages!

What is your favourite language?

My native language – Latvian – is my favourite. Latvia is so small and its relationship with other nations has historically been so delicate, that the Latvian language has often come under threat from the bigger countries that have ruled us.

What language do you most want to learn?

I want to continue my English studies and become fluent. I also have a dream of learning Japanese. And I would be happy if I knew Spanish, Finland and Latin!

I actually have a poem about knowing all the different kinds of languages – including the languages of dogs, horses, cats, ants, flamingos, dolphins, cows, elephants, beetles... Then I can ask all three of my cats what time will they arrive for breakfast, and ask dolphins what they see in their dreams!

About the illustrator

Chein Shyan Lee is an illustrator based in Malaysia. She is a graduate of Birmingham City University, with a BA (Hons) in Visual Communications, specialising in illustration.

Her interests include children's book illustration, editorial, reportage drawing, branding, printmaking and embroidery. Her work reflects her persistence and attention to detail.

Her illustrations featured in *Once Upon A Time In Birmingham: Women Who Dared To Dream*, a collection of real-life stories about inspirational Birmingham women, published by the Emma Press in 2018.

You can find her on Instagram @cheinshyan.

About the translator

Žanete Vēvere Pasqualini works as a literary agent for the Latvian Literature platform and translates in her spare time.

Her translation of Kristine Ulberga's *The Green Crow* was published by Peter Owen Publishers in 2018, and she translated the stories 'The Birds of Ķīpsala Island' by Dace Rukšāne and 'The Shakes' by Svens Kuzmins for *The Book of Riga*, published by Comma Press in 2018, as well as 'The Quarry' by Jana Egle for *Words Without Borders* magazine.

Her other translations in English include: *The Noisy Classroom* by Ieva Flamingo (children's poetry, published by the Emma Press in 2017), *Dog Town* by Luīze Pastore (a children's book, published by Firefly Press in 2018), and the forthcoming Bicki-Books poetry series for children (Emma Press, 2019). Žanete is currently working on translating *The Room*, a novel by Laima Kota.

AN INTERVIEW WITH ŽANETE

How many languages do you speak?

I speak English, Italian and Russian well. I have some basic knowledge of French, and I get by in German. I've studied Spanish and Finnish, too, but I haven't used these languages for so long that I've practically lost them.

What's the best part of being a translator?

The best part of being the translator is 'plunging' into a different culture while trying to deliver a story, a message, an atmosphere or feel of the work in question and a far-away place, bringing two cultures together.

I love the challenge of preserving the particularities that might be interesting to a foreign audience, keeping in some nuances of the original language but also editing out what might obstruct the fluency of the text in the translation.

What languages do you wish you could speak?

I'm a little like Lela in 'The Girl Who Learned All The Languages Of The World' because almost every time I travel I want to learn the language of the country I'm visiting!

Language is a gate to the culture of a nation and I love learning about our world, although I think trying to learn all the languages of the world all at once would be a big mistake. You have to choose which languages you want to study very carefully and try learning them as well as you can, or you'll end up not speaking any language well.

Lately, my life is very hectic and busy and there are times when I'm particularly tired, whilst speaking a foreign language, and I start making mistakes and it annoys me enormously as I'm immediately aware of it.

Right now, I wish I could speak Arabic as I've just returned from the United Arab Emirates where I took part in the SIBF Publisher's Conference. It was an amazing and enriching experience and, back in my hotel after a very busy day, I loved switching on a local TV channel and just watching the news and a TV series that was on every evening at the same time.

Even though I didn't speak the language, I somehow had a feeling it brought me closer to their culture and I could relate to them. I love listening to languages I don't understand and trying to guess what the topic is.

I would definitely like to improve my French and German, becoming fluent, possibly without a foreign accent (which is practically impossible, I believe). Perhaps I'd like to learn Swedish as well, as they are our neighbours. I've always had difficulty in limiting my choices, I want too much and struggle to see that it would have been better to do something less but well, I still keep trying to do it all.

Still, I wouldn't be ready to give up any of the languages I speak already, or on wishing to speak even more languages.

What is your favourite language?

I love all the languages I speak. It's a little like asking which is your favourite child. However, apart from my native language, English has a very special place in my heart as it was my first foreign language and it gave me the feeling that the whole world was in my pocket. English gave me freedom.

I could read, travel, talk to people. I learnt English when Latvia was still under Soviet domination so its role was even more significant. At first it was a greater freedom of my mind, then it was also a freedom to move in the world and discover new countries and cultures.

WRITE YOUR OWN STORY

Fancy writing your own story and then maybe illustrating it too? Editor **Charlotte Geater** has come up with some ideas to help get you started.

Try using some of the new words you've learned from the languages in this book in stories of your own! How about writing about a holiday, or about travelling the world?

If you could learn any language in the world, what would it be? Write a story about what you could do if you knew this language!

What would it be like if you could suddenly speak and understand every language in the world? What would you do first?

Have you ever wished that you could talk to animals? Write a story about what it would be like if you could suddenly understand the language of pigeons, or dogs, or every animal you saw!

Have you ever misheard something that someone has said to you? Write a story about how confusing it can be when this happens!

If aliens visited earth, would we be able to understand them? Would they be able to speak to us? Write about what you think talking to an alien would look like!

See if you can find a bilingual dictionary, or a dictionary that will let you look up words in another language (such as English to French, or English to Latvian!) – a library should be able to help you with this.

Look up your favourite words in this dictionary and copy out the translations. What do these words remind you of now? What do they sound like? What do they look like? What do they feel like? Write a story based on these words!

We'd love to see what you come up with in response to these prompts! If you'd like us to take a look, email your poems and pictures to hello@theemmapress.com with 'The Girl Who Learned' in the subject line.

TRANSLATION STATION

Translating books from one language into another is a real art, not least when the book itself is about translation! We asked translator **Žanete Vēvere Pasqualini** to tell us a bit about her experience of translating the book. Here's what she said...

Translation isn't just about changing one word for another. Sometimes languages have different forms of words, depending on the gender of the person being spoken about, and there are lots of other reasons why a word might look different depending on the other words around it.

Latvian has a very complex syntax, which means the way we organise our sentences. We use long and complicated sentences that often have to be split up and re-organised when translated into other languages.

Where possible, I always try to compensate for any idiomatic expressions which are then lost. Some expressions are brighter in Latvian, some in English, so it's great if you are able to see an opportunity to enrich the text wherever it can be done.

I think wordplay is definitely the trickiest part of the translation. Sometimes I do manage to find a decent substitute, but sometimes it's just not possible and I'm forced to edit some things out, but it's always a painful choice to make.

I would like to give you some examples of the difficulties I encountered with *The Girl Who Learned All The Languages Of The World*. So, for example:

★ On page 6, Lela's mum explains to her: 'Mixing up words like "elevator" and "waiter" like you did just now is a common mistake if you don't speak English very well.' The wordplay in Lela's mistake (*elevator* sounding like *waiter*) was easy to translate, as it already referred to the English language, but now it sounds slightly weird as the text is in English now.

★ On page 17, Grandma Primrose comes to visit Lela. In Latvian, the grandma's name was Ieva, which is – in Latvian – the name of a blooming bird-cherry tree as well as the name of the first woman on earth (Eve, in English). There was also a reference to the first woman on earth in the original text.

I chose to name Lela's grandma Primrose and keep the reference to the first flowers of spring, as I felt the image of a flower was quite important. I could have chosen to name Lela's grandmother Eve and keep the reference to the first woman on earth, but something had to be given up, so I didn't.

★ The same thing also happened on page 39, with Mary Jane's leaflet about her missing rabbit Pink, where she seems to say that Pink is fond of *sliekas*, which translates as 'earthworms' in English. And then Lela learns that Mary Jane was actually mentioning a reward that wouldn't be *lieks* or 'redundant'.

To make the *sliekas/lieks* confusion work, the text had to be changed. So I kept the reference to earthworms and took it further away, to some wordplay about making one's heart warm: 'What is says is that you'll get an ice cream as a reward, to warm your heart. *Heart warm*, not *earthworm!*'

About the Emma Press

The Emma Press is an independent publishing house based in the Jewellery Quarter, Birmingham, UK. We specialise in poetry, short fiction and children's books.

The Emma Press won the Michael Marks Award for Poetry Pamphlet Publishers in 2016 and Emma Press books have won the Poetry Book Society Pamphlet Choice Award, the Saboteur Award for Best Collaborative Work, and CLiPPA, the CLPE award for children's poetry books.

We publish themed poetry anthologies, single-author poetry and fiction pamphlets (chapbooks), and books for children. We have a growing list of translations which includes titles from Latvia, Estonia, Indonesia, Spain and the Netherlands.

We run regular calls for submissions, and try to do as many events as possible, from book-launch parties to writing workshops to school visits. You can find out more about the Emma Press and buy books directly from us here:

theemmapress.com

The Noisy Classroom

Poems by Ieva Flamingo
Illustrated by Vivianna Maria Staņislavska
Translated by Žanete Vēvere Pasqualini,
Sara Smith and Richard O'Brien

It isn't easy being a kid – especially not in the noisiest class in the school. Some days, you struggle with algebra, or too much homework. Sometimes, one of your fellow pupils just won't SHUT UP. When the class feels like a many-headed dragon, how can you find a place for yourself? Would you feel less lonely if you could smuggle a cat in?

£8.50

Hardback ISBN 978-1-910139-82-0
A collection of poems aimed at children aged 8+

ALSO FROM THE EMMA PRESS

Once Upon A Time In Birmingham
Women Who Dared To Dream

Stories by Louise Palfreyman. Illustrations by Jan Bowman, Yasmin Bryan, Amy Louise Evans, Saadia Hipkiss, Chein Shyan Lee, Farah Osseili & Michelle Turton

Who was the world's first female programmer? Who made history as the first British woman to sail solo around the world non-stop? Who is Birmingham's first female Muslim MP? Meet Mary Lee Berners-Lee, Lisa Clayton, Shabana Mahmood and many more in this a lively introduction to thirty of Birmingham's most awe-inspiring women, past and present.

£14.99
Hardback ISBN 978-1-910139-82-0
Stories about real-life women aimed at children aged 11+

ALSO FROM THE EMMA PRESS

Everyone's the Smartest

Poems by Contra, illustrated by Ulla Saar. Translated from Estonian by Charlotte Geater, Kätlin Kaldmaa & Richard O'Brien

School can be hard, fun and strange – sometimes all at once. It's full of your best friends and all the teachers as well as lots of kids you haven't met. Every day reveals more stories and challenges... *Everyone's the Smartest* is a collection of poems which tell strange new stories in familiar settings. From clever ducks who fly far away while children are stuck in school, to bathroom taps that are just one mistake away from turning the school into a great lake, this collection reminds its readers that there is wonder everywhere.

£12.00
Paperback ISBN 978-1-910139-99-8
Poems aimed at children aged 8+

The Book of Clouds

**Poems by Juris Kronbergs, illustrated by Anete Melece
Translated from Latvian by Mara Rozitis & Richard O'Brien**

If you look up on a cloudy day, you'll see a whole new surprising world above you – the world of clouds! *The Book of Clouds* is an introduction to this world – and the guide you'll want by your side to help you understand it.

A mix of dreamy fantasy and scientific fact, this is the perfect gift for any child with their head stuck in the clouds – and for anyone who has ever wondered what's up there in the skies above. This book is ideal for children to use as a starting point for their own imaginative creative play.

£12.00

Hardback ISBN 978-1-910139-14-1
Poems aimed at children aged 8+